THREE of SWORDS

THE TAROT
TRILOGY
BOOK ONE

J.D. BRETTON

THREE OF SWORDS

THE TAROT TRILOGY, BOOK ONE

J.D. Bretton

Three of Swords, The Tarot Trilogy, Book One

By J.D. Bretton

Copyright © 2016 J.D. Bretton

This is a work of fiction. Names, characters, businesses, places, events, and incidents are the products of the author's imagination or are used in a fictitious manner. Any resemblance to actual persons, living or dead, or actual events is purely coincidental.

Printed in the United States of America

First Printing, 2016

Splintered Sky Publishing

ISBN: 9780692655337

Cover Design by Fiona Jayde
Interior Design by The Deliberate Page

For B.K.-

Thanks for the push

"There is real love just as there are real ghosts; every person speaks of it, few persons have seen it."

François de la Rochefoucauld

CHAPTER 1

Ten weeks of vacation stretched before Danielle like a slowly unwinding ribbon. No schedules, commitments, or obligations. The summer of love, her husband Matt liked to say — such a typical male. Danielle looked forward to all the time to work on their new house and to getting back to her painting. After packing up her room today, she had left school just as eagerly as her students had a few hours earlier.

As she drove home, the heat shimmered off the asphalt. This summer would sizzle if the past few weeks were any indication of the months to come.

But as much as she would enjoy the time off, this summer would be different. A thread of sadness wove its way through each day since she and Matt lost their baby two months ago. Lost; such an inaccurate euphemism, as if she had been carelessly misplaced, like the car keys or someone's glasses.

It had started out perfectly. When Danielle had been four months along, they had painted the baby's room a pale yellow, the color of the morning sun. She had tucked each tiny outfit carefully in the drawers. A few presents from family and friends decorated the shelves. Two previous miscarriages had made them cautious, but their days filled with hopes and plans for the future as Danielle's body stirred with the first small flutters of movement. When the time came for the ultrasound, they could hardly contain their excitement, anxious to get a glimpse of the tiny human they had created. On the examining room table in her crinkly paper gown, Danielle vibrated with anticipation. The technician spread gel over her belly and rolled the instrument over the swell of the new life inside her.

At first, Danielle did not comprehend when the technician said she couldn't find the heartbeat. Couldn't find the heartbeat? She got her answer when she saw Matt's face. As the meaning of the words finally sank in, Danielle broke down. Each inhale tore at her chest like broken glass. And soon after, it ended. A visit to the hospital, endless excruciating explanations to relatives and friends, and a door closed forever.

At that moment, her world shifted. Nothing would ever be the same again. Most people could not understand the strength of her sorrow or how she longed for the child who had just disappeared. She even hung up on her mother who had the nerve to imply that she might have caused the miscarriage because she had been so anxious about the pregnancy. "Try yoga," her mother had advised.

The sadness after each loss had expanded throughout her whole body. Some days, it totally engulfed her. She and Matt each dealt with it in different ways. Matt just wanted to move on, not talk about it, and get past it. Danielle needed to go over every detail again and again, searching for the moment when things went wrong. It had led to some of the worst fights in their five years of marriage.

But no one, not even Matt, knew the one secret that she had held close for the last few months. She knew he would think it was foolish. He teased her about her belief in premonitions and karma, and made fun of how she dabbled in tarot cards. In the past, a few of Danielle's dreams had come true, but she usually dismissed these as just coincidences. This time had been different.

A few weeks before the miscarriage, Danielle had a powerful and vivid dream. A toddler with blonde curls cascading down her back, and the same green eyes as Danielle, perched on their bed. As she continued to watch, the image shimmered and distorted, as if she observed everything through the glass of a fun house mirror or underwater. The child held her arms out, but Danielle froze.

"I can't stay," the child whispered. As Danielle reached out, the image flickered and fluttered like the reel of an old movie, and then went dark. The vision of the child echoed in her memory. She believed that the dream was somehow real, a premonition.

Danielle shook her head. She needed to keep her focus on the present, and on the road. She needed to be more practical and logical, like Matt. If it weren't for him, they wouldn't have bought their house almost a year ago. Although Danielle had fallen in love the first time she had walked through the door of the old colonial, the house's history made her nervous.

According to the real estate agent, a man named Xavier Hawthorne died mysteriously in the house three years ago. It had been vacant since then, too many potential buyers scared off by the stories. But Matt jumped at the price, and they moved in two months later. On the outskirts of town, they owned a few acres of property, most of it woods, but still close enough to downtown and a train ride away from New York City.

Danielle pulled into the driveway, glad to finally be home. She dropped her bags in the hallway and grabbed a bottle of wine on her way to the kitchen. She had just enough time to relax and take a shower before she and Matt needed to be at their friend Karen's house for a "start of the summer" party. She poured herself a glass of wine, opened a box of crackers, and sank down in her favorite chair. Closing her eyes, she sipped her wine and savored the feel of the cool glass against her lips. The dark liquid swirled against her tongue. With each swallow, her body softened and opened. She drifted as the pleasant haze of alcohol lulled her to sleep.

Danielle started when she felt a slow trace of fingers burn a path across her cheek. She turned her head and gently parted her mouth, expecting to be greeted by Matt's full lips pressed against hers. She opened her eyes, surprised to find herself alone. Nothing stirred in the room except for the slow wave of the curtains ruffled by the wind. *I must have drunk more than I thought*, she mused, as she viewed the almost empty bottle on the table.

When she looked at the clock, she realized that she had dozed off for an hour. She needed to get in the shower if they had any hopes of getting to the party on time. She rose from the chair, still groggy from sleep and wine, and walked up to the master bathroom.

The hazy late afternoon sunlight drifted through the open window. Wisps of clouds crept across the sky. Danielle undressed, happy to shed her work clothes, and looked forward to a summer filled with flip-flops and sundresses. The cool tile felt delicious under her feet. The breeze washed over her skin.

In the shower, the warm water flowed over her body. She ran her hands down her face and her arms. Despite her annoyance with her mother, she had taken up yoga and it had made her body lean and toned. Her hands skimmed down her breasts, and her nipples hardened under her touch. As her hands slid farther, down to her flat belly, her thoughts wandered to Matt.

She imagined his mouth tracing circles with his tongue on her nipples. Her hand dropped and found the folds between her legs. A delicious ache stirred in her lower belly and a slickness swelled between her thighs. With one hand braced against the shower wall, and the other between her legs, her fingers vibrated faster and faster until she released in a shudder. Her body arched. But just as quickly, her satisfaction faded as she fantasized about Matt hard inside her, his lanky runner's body wrapped around her.

She and Matt had met in college. He had immediately swept her off her feet. Matt could charm anyone with his mischievous smile and easy manner. He had been a big flirt when they met, and he still was. Matt could talk to anyone anywhere and have them believe he was their best friend. A large part of what made him successful as a sales rep for Novocom Pharmaceuticals was that he could sell anything to anyone.

They were complete opposites. Matt was the life of the party, the jock, the quintessential all-American boy, while Danielle, an artist, preferred to stay at home with her books and a few close friends. He embodied everything she wasn't and most of the time that made them fit together like connected puzzle pieces, complete. But lately, Matt spent a lot of time traveling for his job, which often left Danielle alone. He was leaving for a business conference in Las Vegas tomorrow and would be gone for a week. She didn't usually mind the quiet, but she worried about being alone with her grief without the distraction of work. The front door slammed.

"I'm home, where are you?" Matt shouted up the stairs.

"Up here, just getting ready." *We might just have to be late for the party,* thought Danielle. She threw a towel around herself and met Matt as he bounded up the stairs.

"Naked and wet, just the way I like you." Matt smirked with his boyish grin as he embraced her. She wound her arms around his neck and burrowed her head in his sculpted shoulder. The towel dropped between them to the floor. His hands trailed down her back while he gently kissed her neck. His hardness pressed against her and she reached down to unbutton his pants.

"Not so fast. I have plans for you." Matt scooped her up and tossed her on the bed.

"What did you have in mind?" Danielle gazed into his piercing blue eyes and ruffled his short brown hair.

"Let's try this first." Matt raised her hands above her head and coaxed her to hold onto the railing of the bed. Exposed and vulnerable, she lay naked on the bed while he towered above her, fully clothed. Every cell of her skin tingled with anticipation. He knelt next to her and slowly caressed her breasts with his supple hands. He grasped one of her nipples between his thumb and finger and tugged and rolled her nipple until she moaned with pleasure. She closed her eyes to drink in the sensation.

Then his mouth covered her nipple. He sucked and playfully bit her until her hips rose. His hand slid down her belly and expertly parted her legs. One finger traced over her lips.

"God, you're so wet." He made small circles with his thumb while his finger pulsed in and out, in and out. She tightened against his finger.

"Come on, baby," Matt whispered as he licked her nipples. His finger moved faster, penetrated her again and again until with a cry, she clenched against him and shuddered with pleasure.

Matt then rose and took off his pants. His erection pulsed. As he moved between her legs, Danielle grasped his penis and guided him inside her. She was filled with exquisite sensations. She wrapped her legs around him and twisted his shirt in her hands. He drove into her, thrust after thrust, until they both came hard against each other, breathless. Matt slipped off and lay next to her. His hand draped protectively over her stomach.

"Well, that was fantastic, Mrs. Williams. You are so beautiful."

Danielle sighed. "Do we really have to go to the party? This is so much nicer, don't you think?" She relaxed her head into the pillow and pictured a quiet night on the couch snuggled next to Matt.

"Come on, everyone's expecting us." Matt yanked the blankets from her and tickled her.

"Okay, okay, stop!" Danielle implored. "I'm getting up." Just then, her phone rang. She reached over. Her friend Karen's name lit up the screen. "Hey, Karen."

"Where the hell are you guys? Everyone's wondering where you are. Are you still coming?"

"Yeah, we'll be there in half an hour or so. Matt got home late from work. Do you need anything?"

"Can you pick up some ice on your way over, and wine if you want it. I know how picky you are."

"Sure, see you in a bit."

She quickly showered again while Matt dozed on the bed. After she woke Matt up for his turn cleaning up, she dressed in her favorite pair of jeans and a tank top, and tipped her head to artfully mess her cropped blonde hair. Staring into the bedroom mirror, she put on mascara and lip gloss. *Not bad for five minutes*, thought Danielle. Never considering herself beautiful, she had been plagued with being called cute since she was young. Her five-foot-two stature didn't help. Her gray-green eyes had to be her best feature, large and rimmed with long lashes that stood out against her pale skin. People usually commented on her eyes when they met her, that and her ass, according to Matt.

Before heading downstairs, she pulled her tarot deck from the drawer of her nightstand. Her college roommate had given her the deck as a birthday present many years ago. Danielle occasionally picked it up when she needed guidance or inspiration. Definitely an amateur, she still needed to flip through one of her books to interpret the meaning. She equated it to reading horoscopes in the newspaper. She knew that thought would offend her former roommate who insisted that interpreting the images was an art form and that the cards hardly ever meant the same thing.

After shuffling them, she cut the deck and pulled out a card—the Lovers. That boded well for the summer. Although she'd never paid much attention to them before, she noticed the red wings and flaming hair of Cupid. The lovers were separated by a mountain and dark clouds. *Not so romantic after all*, thought Danielle. She left the card and the deck on her nightstand and went to find Matt.

He waited for her at the door looking gorgeous, his hair still wet from the shower. "Are you ready?" He reached out his hand to pull her closer. "We could always stay home." His hard penis pressed against her.

"So now you like my idea?" Danielle smiled. "You know we have to go. I just told Karen we would be there."

"I know, but later you and I have some unfinished business."

CHAPTER 2

When they arrived at the party, their friends greeted them with shouts. "Now the party's started; Matt's here!"

Danielle often thought that if they ever got a divorce, Matt would definitely get all their friends. Danielle hadn't expected to see so many people at the party. The kitchen buzzed with the already tipsy crowd of Karen and Brian's friends. Matt disappeared to socialize. Danielle knew that she would probably not see him again until she was ready to leave and had to drag him off to go home.

Karen, effortlessly gorgeous as usual with her long black hair pulled back into a ponytail, gave Danielle a hug. "You look like you need a big glass of wine. Give me that bottle."

"Hey, Danielle!" Brian shouted from across the room. Danielle waved to him and reached for the glass of wine that Karen handed her. She wasn't sure she should be drinking again, considering the nearly empty bottle of wine from this afternoon, but she needed to celebrate her first night of summer vacation.

"Come on," Karen said. "Brenda and Angela are out on the porch."

Danielle settled into a spot on the wicker couch on the porch. Under the twinkling lights strung across the ceiling, she prepared to spend the rest of the night drinking and catching up with the girls.

As the evening wore on, Danielle's head started to spin from all the wine. With blurry eyes, she searched the room for Matt. She thought about getting up, but worried that her drunken legs would not cooperate. It was definitely time to go home.

Karen interrupted her train of thought. "Danielle, what about you?"

"Sorry, what?"

"If you could have a free pass with anyone, who would it be?"

"Definitely Bradley Cooper," said Angela. "Those eyes, he could do anything he wanted with me."

"Dwayne Johnson," Karen added. "That body, I would ride him like a pony!"

"Eew! He's so old!" Brenda exclaimed. "Robert Pattinson for me."

"Oh my God, Brenda, that's just because you're a Twilight fan, vampire girl."

"Okay Danielle, fess up, who's your free pass?"

"I don't know. I can't really think of anyone."

As Danielle squirmed under the pressure to respond, the men descended upon the girls' conversation. Matt sat on the arm of Danielle's chair.

"What's going on, ladies?"

"We're discussing who we would fuck if we weren't tied down to you schmucks. Your wife can't seem to think of anyone, so you must be sticking it to her pretty good!" Karen's directness sent the group into peals of laughter, but Danielle's cheeks reddened in embarrassment.

"You got that right." Matt grinned at Danielle.

"Since we have all of you here, Kevin and I have an announcement to make," said Brenda, a serious look on her usually carefree face. Danielle ran through the list of possible scenarios in her head. Brenda and Kevin had dated for over a year—moving in together, marriage, relocating for a new job?

"We're going to have a baby," blurted Brenda, as if she was trying to say the words before she could pull them back in and make them untrue.

"You're shitting us!" Brian said.

"Is it a baby vampire?" joked Angela.

"Congratulations, drinks all around, except for you, Brenda. I wondered why you weren't the lush you usually are."

Danielle's face immediately fell. She should be happy for her friend, but the wound inside her chest just got a little bigger. *A baby? They aren't even married. They hadn't even planned to have a family. It should be me. Why couldn't it be me?*

Karen's perceptive eyes met hers. "Danielle, come and help me in the kitchen."

Danielle eagerly accepted the offer and stumbled to the kitchen, desperate to escape the rounds of congratulatory toasts.

"I'm sorry. I know this is hard for you," Karen said with concern.

"Yeah, I just need to go. Tell everyone I didn't feel well and tell Matt to meet me at the car." Danielle held back the tears that threatened to spill down her face.

She staggered out into the muggy night air, grateful to close the door behind her and shut out the noise of the party. She got in the passenger seat, tipped her head back against the headrest, and put her hands to her forehead to contain the heartache that seemed to seep from every pore.

Matt opened the car door and slid into the driver's seat.

"What's up? Karen told me you wanted to leave. We're just celebrating Kevin and Brenda's news."

"I just can't," she whispered.

Matt gave her an irritated look. "Listen, I understand, Danielle, but this isn't about you, it's about Brenda and Kevin. You've got to get past this."

"It's not that easy. I just can't pretend that nothing happened, like you can. I need to talk about it. I need to talk about what we're going to do. You always avoid the subject." Tears streamed down her face.

"We've talked. How is talking about it over and over going to help? It's not going to change anything. Maybe we're not meant to have kids. That wouldn't be the end of the world, would it?"

"What? You've never said anything like that before."

"I just can't keep doing this. This isn't good for you. It isn't good for us. You need to figure out how to move on."

Matt pulled out of the driveway. They didn't look at each other or speak on the ride home. This had become a familiar argument over the last few months. An argument that no one could win. He couldn't comprehend her need to mourn. Danielle felt unable to lie to herself that nothing had happened, as he preferred to do. She could see no resolution to their situation.

They drove home in silence and entered the house without speaking. Matt retreated to the living room to the empty solace of the TV.

As she walked up to their room, she held onto the wall to steady herself, but still managed to trip on the last step and fall headlong into the wall. "Never drinking this much again," she said as she picked herself up. She attempted to peel off her clothes without tipping over, then threw them onto the floor. She collapsed onto the bed, groaning as the room continued to whirl around her and her head throbbed. As she lay on the bed, she thought she heard the sound of quiet laughter. *Must be the TV*, she thought as she passed out, into oblivion.

CHAPTER 3

The blare of the alarm clock jarred Danielle awake. She had slept fitfully last night, waking a few times when she thought she'd felt Matt's hand on her shoulder. But when she had rolled over to check, the bed was empty. She blearily opened her eyes and groped for the Off button. 5:00 a.m. Matt had to get up to drive to the airport for his flight to Las Vegas. Danielle reached over to shake Matt awake, but he was still not there.

He must have slept on the couch. He can just get himself up, thought Danielle as she stared at the ceiling. Her emotions jumbled together. Anger, sadness, and guilt all warred inside her head as she replayed their fight.

Then she heard the stairs creak. When Matt snuck under the covers, she turned away. She did not want to see his eyes accuse her. Afraid if she looked at him, she would say something she might later regret.

Matt reached his arm across her waist and rested his hand on her stomach. His fingers spread wide. He traced his hand up and down her torso, and grazed the tips of her nipples with his fingertips. His hand traveled down, beneath the band of her underwear.

She wanted to push his hand away, still hurt and angry from last night, but her body responded to his touch.

His penis hardened against her ass. His hand slipped behind her and squeezed her cheeks. His finger entered her and probed the wetness there. In silence, he pushed her onto her stomach and guided her knees underneath. He kneeled behind her and spread her knees wider, not entering her at first.

He reached around her, teasing at the opening of her vagina with his light touch. The throbbing inside her built. He moved his now-wet fingertips to her clitoris as she pushed back against him. She longed for him to be inside her. He let her linger there and caressed her with his fingers until she could no longer bear it. She wanted to scream out to him, grab his cock, and pull it inside her. When she thought she couldn't take another minute, he grasped her thighs and thrust inside her. He drove into her and shuddered in his release as the waves of her orgasm completely overcame her.

They both panted in silence. Matt kissed the back of her head gently, then pulled out of her and got up without speaking. To Danielle, it felt like a goodbye.

She feigned sleep while Matt showered, packed, and left the house. When the front door clicked shut and she heard his car start in the driveway, she got up and went to the window. She hoped he would look up at her, stop the car, come back inside, and tell her everything was okay. But he just drove off.

Danielle stood at the window and stared at the empty driveway in shock.

Her head pounded from her hangover. *Coffee*, Danielle thought. *I need lots of coffee.* She pulled on an old pair of sweatpants and a sports bra, then padded downstairs to the kitchen. She saw a note from Matt on the counter.

We both need some time to think.

I'm going to stay a few extra days after the conference and visit Frank.

We'll talk when I get back.

Love,
Matt

Hmph, thought Danielle, *so you get to decide what we both need. What a jerk.* As much as she loved Matt, he always thought he knew what was best for both of them. Maybe this time apart was a good thing. Maybe she did need to think about what an ass he was being and why he just couldn't be more understanding. *This is getting me nowhere,* Danielle thought as she sipped her coffee. She needed a plan to get herself through today.

She really should unpack some of the boxes left over from when they moved into the house. They had shoved them up in the attic and never found the time to finish the job. Danielle had never even taken out her sketchbooks, pencils, and paints. Maybe that's what she needed. Although she taught art, she hadn't made time for her own projects for quite a while.

She ate an apple for breakfast and decided to do some yoga first to take her mind off Matt's note. She threw her mat down on the living room floor and searched on her tablet for a class. She found one named "Rise and Shine." *Perfect*, thought Danielle. Yoga relaxed her to the point where she often drifted off to sleep in savasana, the corpse pose. She followed the class through sun salutations, chaturanga, and the half-moon pose. The hypnotic voice of the instructor and the music comforted her. The instructor gave directions for the last pose, savasana, the corpse…

"Take this time to close your eyes. Place your arms wide out to the sides, palms face up. Take a slow deep breath, shoulders release back and down. Legs out in front, feet wide, and feel your body sink into the floor. As you exhale, give yourself permission to completely relax. To heal means to surrender. When you love yourself, you heal yourself. Take some deep breaths, let yourself sink deeper and deeper into relaxation."

Focused on the steady rhythm of her breath, Danielle fell into a semiconscious state. She had a heightened awareness of her body. The air tingled against her skin as her muscles sank into the floor. Suddenly, she felt the weight of hands run down the sides of her face, her neck, and the length of her arms. *I must be dreaming*. The hands swept lower. She shivered when they reached the bare skin of her waist and continued across her hips and down her thighs. Her heart fluttered like a moth's wings against glass.

Then the hands pressed her shoulders up and back. Her chest rose as soft lips brushed gently against hers, hesitated, and then pulled away. Danielle opened her eyes.

A face shimmered above her. Dark wavy hair spilled across black eyes. The smoldering eyes penetrated her own with an unwavering confidence and a hint of surprise. A scruff of a beard spread across sculpted cheekbones. His lips parted. A tattoo of a wing curled down the side of his neck and led to a bare chest.

The buzz of the cellphone on the counter jolted Danielle, and the image above her dissolved like a reflection in water that slowly rippled away. Danielle lay there for a minute as her heart beat wildly, unsure of what just happened. She got up unsteadily and grabbed her phone.

"Hi, Karen." Danielle's voice quavered.

"I'm just checking in on you after last night. Is everything okay? You don't sound so good."

"I'm all right, just a little hung over. And Matt and I got into a fight last night. He left without even saying goodbye."

"I'm so sorry. You know how his temper can be. He'll come around and be apologizing all over the place by the time he gets to Las Vegas."

"I don't know. This time was different. I'm not sure if I'd even forgive him."

"Let's go have lunch, some girl time. We can talk."

"Thanks, but I think I'm just going to stay home. I have some things to do. I just don't feel like going out."

"Are you sure? Text me if you change your mind. I'm worried about you."

"Don't worry, I'll be fine. I'll text you later." Danielle's head swam. Whose face had she just seen? What deep part of her subconscious had she pulled that from? She did not recognize him. She ran through possible connections in her mind—actor, singer, stranger she passed in the street, or some creation of her own erotic psyche?

Her imagination certainly conjured up a devastatingly gorgeous figment, those dark brooding eyes, and the tattoo — definitely a bad boy. *Oh my God, I'm fantasizing about a dream, how pathetic.* Maybe she missed Matt more than she thought. She contemplated calling him, but didn't know what she would say. Definitely not, "I'm sorry."

Danielle pushed away her memories of last night's argument with Matt and decided to get to work in the attic. She climbed the steep stairs and entered the cavernous space. The wood plank floor ran the entire length of the house. The rafters stretched overhead like the ribs of a giant animal. Danielle plunked down in the middle of the boxes stacked haphazardly on the floor.

She opened the first box, which contained Matt's track trophies and awards from college and high school. *Those can stay right where they are*, Danielle thought as she closed the box. The next box overflowed with clothes that needed to take a trip to Goodwill. A third yielded her sketchbooks, drawing pencils, paints, and brushes. She hadn't painted or sketched anything for months. She curved her hand across the frayed edges of one of her sketchbooks, then flipped through the pages. Each drawing linked to a memory like an old friend. She placed it back in the box and carried it to the stairwell.

Wiping the sweat from her forehead, she returned to the stack of boxes. As the sun beat down on the roof, the temperature rose. She walked to one of the windows on the far side of the attic to see if she could open it and circulate the air. As she pushed up against the window to get it to budge, she noticed a brown envelope wedged between the edge of the floorboard and the wall.

She pulled the envelope from the floor and saw that it was addressed to Xavier Hawthorne. The return address named an art gallery in New York. Danielle was intrigued. She didn't know anything about their house's former occupant other than his untimely death at a young age. This must have been left behind when they had emptied the house of all his belongings. Feeling only slightly guilty, she opened the envelope and read the letter inside.

Cotter Gallery
214 West 22nd Street
New York, New York

May 21, 2012

Dear Mr. Hawthorne,

Enclosed please find promotional materials for your upcoming exhibition at the Cotter Gallery. We look forward to seeing you opening night on June 30th.

Sincerely,
Abby Wilson
Gallery Coordinator

She hadn't realized he was an artist. The next sheet of paper contained a bio with a few photographs. Danielle read:

Xavier Hawthorne is a graduate of Rhode Island School of Design. His photography has garnered several awards, including the honor of being a finalist for the 2011 Discovery of the Year International Photography Award.

His black-and-white photography captures the essence of humanity by elevating the everyday to the extraordinary through the interaction of his subjects with time, light, and the environment.

To the right of his bio were three black-and-white photographs. The first showed a picture of a crowded street corner. Everyone stared straight ahead or down at their cell phones except for one woman whose head tilted toward the sky. In the second picture, a man and a woman walked in opposite directions on the sidewalk. The third picture zoomed in on a tiny hand stretched into a shaft of light. An undertone of sadness linked all three.

She slid the next paper in the packet to the top. It was a self-portrait. Danielle's eyes widened in disbelief and a shudder ran down her spine. The face from her dream this morning looked back at her. The same powerful dark eyes, the wave of hair across his forehead, the tattoo of a wing that wrapped around his neck. It can't be. *What is going on?* She wavered from one theory to the next. She must have seen a picture of him in the news or in a magazine. Something must have triggered her crazy vision this morning.

She needed to get out of the house. She stuffed the papers in the envelope and bolted down the stairs, grateful to close the attic door behind her. She immediately texted Karen.

I changed my mind. Let's meet for lunch.

CHAPTER 4

Karen met her downtown at the Metro Café. Late as usual, Karen flew into the restaurant with her signature bluntness.

"You do not look good. You look like you've seen a ghost."

"Well, now that you mention it, what do you know about Xavier Hawthorne?" Danielle pushed the envelope across the table. Karen had grown up in Fairview and seemed to know everyone and everything in this town.

"Where did you find this?" asked Karen as she perused the contents of the envelope.

"In the attic. It must have been left behind."

"Definitely a hottie, wasn't he?" Karen waved the portrait in front of her. "Too bad someone murdered him."

Danielle raised her eyebrows.

"Yeah, I forget you live under a rock. You really need to get out more, watch the news, there's this invention called a TV."

Danielle just rolled her eyes. Her friends teased her constantly for not knowing about the latest TV shows.

"Whatever, isn't it sacrilegious to talk about someone who is dead like that?"

"Lighten up. You know he's totally your type, tortured artist and all. While we're on the subject of hotties, have you heard from that shit husband of yours?"

"No, and I don't want to talk about it. Back to Mr. Hawthorne, please."

"It was all over the news when it happened. It was this big unsolved mystery. Up-and-coming artist shot in his own house, no witnesses, no weapon. They didn't find the body for three days. He was a loner, spent most of his time in New York doing his photography thing. No one ever really saw him around Fairview. No wife, no kids, no girlfriend, no friends in town. His parents are hotshot lawyers in Los Angeles and he's got a younger brother who is apparently a real fuck-up. That's about all that I know other than they had a hell of time selling that house until you guys came along."

After that, their conversation switched to more mundane topics and their long lunch segued into a manicure and shopping. After a few hours away from the house, Danielle's memories of this morning seemed distant and forgettable. She convinced herself that what had happened earlier today was the result of an overactive imagination.

On their way to the parking garage, Karen pulled Danielle down a side street.

"One last stop. Here we are."

A small hole in the wall storefront stood before them. A sign propped up in the window read, "Intuitions: tarot and palm readings, walk-ins welcome."

"I know how much you like this stuff, always playing with that deck of cards of yours. It'll be fun. Maybe we'll get some good news." Karen led her into the shop.

The door jingled as they entered. Couches and chairs, bookshelves, and books sprawled randomly everywhere in dusty chaos. From the back room, an older woman emerged. She had a kind face, wire-rimmed glasses, and piles of gray curly hair that framed her face.

"Well, hello there, my dears. What can I do for you?" A smile lit up her plump face.

"We both would like a tarot reading. This one could use some good news." Karen pointed to Danielle.

"I can only tell the story that I see. Come, sit down." She led them to a table flanked by wooden chairs in the center of the room. "I usually charge twenty-five dollars a reading, but for you ladies today, a special, thirty for both of you."

"Sounds great," replied Danielle.

"Now where are my cards?" The woman searched through one of the bookshelves behind her until she came up with the deck and sat down across from them. "So, my name is Nancy and who are you?" she inquired as she shuffled the cards.

"My name's Danielle and this is Karen."

The woman stopped and held her gaze for a few uncomfortable seconds. Then her affable smile returned as she continued to shuffle the cards. She turned toward Karen.

"Let's start with you, my dear. I want you to hold the deck in your hands so it can absorb your energy."

"Sure thing." Karen glanced out of the corner of her eye at Danielle and raised her eyebrows slightly. Danielle knew Karen was doing this solely for her benefit and did not believe in it one bit. She just shrugged and smiled back at Karen.

"So the tarot will tell us a story. It's a map of our mental and spiritual pathways." She took the deck from

Karen's hands and cut it. She then placed three cards upside down on the table. "Past, present, and future." She tapped the cards from left to right. Nancy then flipped over the card on the left. "Ah, the Eight of Pentacles. You have done hard work to get where you are, laying the groundwork for your career, perhaps? And your present, the Knight of Swords—fierce, determined, you will stop at nothing to pursue your goals. Be careful with that, my dear," Nancy admonished in a motherly tone. "And your future, the Six of Cups. Interesting. Someone may need your help and kindness. You are not quite the cold fish some may think."

Karen and Danielle both burst out laughing. Charlatan or not, Nancy had pretty much characterized Karen in a nutshell.

"Now you, my dear." Nancy gathered the deck to shuffle it and then placed it in Danielle's hands. This time Nancy held her own hands over Danielle's for a few moments before retrieving the deck. "So let's see what the message is for you today." Nancy placed three cards on the table. "Three of Swords. Someone has hurt you, broken your heart. This has made it difficult for you to move on. It's holding you back."

The familiar ache in Danielle's chest returned as she reflected on the losses she had endured and her situation with Matt.

"On to the present, the center of power in your life. The Moon. This symbolizes mystery, the subconscious, and dreams. Pay attention to your dreams, my dear. They may be the path to help you move on from whatever has hurt you. Don't dismiss what your subconscious tries to tell you. And the future…"

Danielle held her breath. She craved something that would give her some hope. Nancy turned the card over. Danielle sighed and shook her head as she saw the card — Death.

"What? What's up with that?" blurted Karen.

"Now, now, this card shows us change, the end of something, perhaps, the beginning of something new, not necessarily death in the physical world. Besides, this is only the direction that things appear to be going at the moment. There is always time to change the path you are on."

Karen grabbed her wallet, switching into her usual protective mode, ready to hustle Danielle out the door.

"Well, thanks, Nancy that was really uplifting," Karen said sarcastically.

"Like I said, my dear, I can only tell the story that I see."

"Thanks, Nancy," said Danielle. As they left, Nancy reached for Danielle's hand.

"Remember what I told you, my dear. You have a strong energy about you that could manifest itself in many ways. Believe what your subconscious shows you."

Danielle just nodded as she tried to make sense of what Nancy told her.

"I'm sorry, Danielle. Not quite the inspiring end to the day that I had planned," said Karen as they walked to their cars.

"Just par for the course. I had fun anyway."

Karen and Danielle hugged goodbye and parted ways in the parking garage. As she started her car to head home, she made a decision. Tomorrow she would pack up everything in the baby's room. She hadn't touched anything there since the miscarriage, and hadn't allowed Matt to, either. Maybe that would give her some closure and allow her to move on. Maybe there was still a chance she could save her marriage.

By the time she arrived at home, the sun was sinking. Shadows bloomed like dark flowers underneath the trees. Ominous clouds covered the sky as the threat of thunderstorms built. The air felt thick and heavy.

The best thing to do would be to call it a day and get a good night's sleep. She would be able to start tomorrow with a new perspective. She grabbed her phone on the chance that Matt would call. As she rummaged through her purse, she saw the envelope that she had brought to show Karen this afternoon. She almost left it, but turned back and brought it upstairs with her.

In the bedroom, she opened the windows wide and hoped a breeze would dispel the stifling heat. She undressed completely. The humid air made even the thought of any clothes unbearable. She lay across the top of the bed, not wanting the weight of the sheet to touch her skin.

Her mind wandered back to Xavier Hawthorne and the dream she'd had this morning. She picked up the envelope from the nightstand by her bed and pulled out the self-portrait. His eyes stared into her soul. She traced her finger along the curve of his cheek down to the tattoo of the wing on his neck. As the storm intensified, the curtains billowed in the wind like fluttering ghosts. Despite the clatter of the rain that had started to fall, Danielle fell into a sound sleep.

A rumble of thunder roused Danielle. She checked her phone for the time. 12:00. She rolled onto her back and closed her eyes, determined to fall back asleep despite the sweltering heat. The rain had not cooled things down at all.

She concentrated on the sound of the rain and her breath. Another loud burst of thunder startled her and she opened her eyes. Lightning splintered the sky and illuminated everything like the flash of a camera. During the next strike of lightning, a silhouette appeared in the corner of the room by the window. She froze. *Must be dreaming, must be dreaming*, Danielle repeated in her head.

The shadow stepped toward her with a cat-like grace. Everything occurred in slow motion. As the apparition sauntered closer, she recognized Xavier Hawthorne's face. His penetrating eyes locked with hers. His form rippled in the dark.

"Definitely dreaming, am I going crazy?" Danielle whispered.

Xavier stopped by the foot of the bed. Danielle's eyes traveled from his eyes to his tattooed neck. He was bare-chested, his jeans slung low on his hips. She lingered on his muscled torso and arms, and his taut abs. *If this is a dream, it's going to be a good one*, Danielle mused. Desire replaced fear.

She saw the same slight surprise mirrored on his face. His mouth turned up in a slow smile as his eyes migrated along the length of her. Her face flushed as he admired every inch of her naked body.

Xavier sat next to her on the bed. She barely felt the weight of his body. He threaded his fingers through her hair. It felt like feathers or a gentle wind. She reached up to touch his face, but he shook his head. The delicate pressure of his hand lowered her arm to the bed. He ran his hand up her arm, continuing up her neck to her face where his thumb traced her open mouth. As the seconds ticked by, the sensations became stronger. He leaned over her. When his lips reached hers, soft and yielding, his tongue gently probed to find hers.

He pulled away, a genuine smile on his face. Danielle's heart beat wildly in her chest. His eyes traveled to her breasts. Her nipples hardened in anticipation of his touch. He bent his head over her. The waves of his black hair brushed her skin. He covered her breasts with kisses, worked around her areolas, then delicately licked the tips of her nipples. As his kisses trailed down her belly, all of her senses awakened. She longed to reach up and touch him, but she did not dare to break the spell of this dream.

Xavier rose and walked to the foot of the bed. He held Danielle's legs and spread them wide as he crawled onto the bed. He trailed his hands up the inside of her thighs, his touch cool against her warm skin. One of his hands held her from behind and lifted her hips. As he lowered his head between her legs, her hips rose to meet his mouth.

His soft lips tingled against her skin. His tongue found her clitoris, circled slowly, then swept down her folds and back up. Her wetness spread with her longing. One of his fingers slipped inside her. As he sucked at her clitoris, his finger pulsed in and out. Her hips rose in rhythm until her body clenched and the shudders of her orgasm convulsed her entire body.

His kisses slowed and he slid next to her on the bed. He reached for her hand and interlaced his fingers in hers. His other hand moved down her face, until her eyes closed. Danielle's chest heaved up and down. She dared not open her eyes, afraid she would open them to an empty room, or much worse, to whoever sat next to her on the bed. Her breathing finally slowed. Her lids felt too heavy to open even if she had wanted to. Before she knew it, she fell into a deep sleep.

CHAPTER 5

Danielle woke when the early morning sunlight streamed through the window. She lay curled on her side with her arms outstretched. Her open palm held the echo of Xavier's hand linked in her own. The memory of last night caused a warm sensation to spread down to her belly. Danielle sighed. "Get hold of yourself, Danielle, only a dream, remember?" she muttered.

She got out of bed, quickly showered, dressed, and ate breakfast. She lingered over her second cup of coffee. Adept at the art of procrastination, she opened up her laptop to check the weather to see if any more storms were forecast for today. On a whim, she typed "ghosts" into the search engine and clicked on the link to a site called *ParanormalExperience.com*. She scrolled through the information.

"People who die in traumatic ways or those who have unfinished business can be bound to the place where they died…ideal conditions for the living to see ghosts are when a person is in a sleepy or meditative state and open to consciousness other than the physical plane…the strength and form that a spirit takes depends on the amount of energy the spirit has gathered…ghosts can and do take physical, solid forms if they have a purpose…there is nothing ethereal and shadowy about them…"

Her mind wandered back to last night. It certainly felt real enough. His lips against her skin, his hands on her body… *This is ridiculous; I need to get a grip on reality.* She shut her laptop. She got a few garbage bags from the kitchen and headed upstairs before she lost her resolve.

Danielle entered the baby's room. Its pale yellow walls no longer created any feeling of calm. Her heart dropped like a stone in her chest. She opened the drawers and tossed the tiny outfits one at a time into the bag. The congratulatory cards, the baby blankets, and the toys piled on top of each other like a morbid cairn. As she threw away one dream after another, tears streamed down her face.

Emotionally spent, she slumped to the floor and hugged the bags to her chest as if she cradled a child. All the guilt she held in, all the pretending that everything was okay, spilled out in endless sobs.

Suddenly a hand touched Danielle's shoulder and a husky voice spoke. "It's all right, Danielle. It will be okay. You are going to be all right."

Danielle leapt to her feet. She backed against the wall and groped on the dresser for the lamp. *I am definitely going off the deep end.* But this was not a dream—Xavier Hawthorne stood between her and the door. She did not dare take her eyes off him. "Don't come any closer. Don't move. I'll call the police." She picked up the lamp, ready to smash it on his head if he came any closer.

"It's okay. I'm not going to hurt you." Xavier approached cautiously with his hands held up in front of him. He looked exactly the way Danielle remembered him from last night. Heat rose to her cheeks as she recalled his lips on her skin.

"Who are you? What are you?" Danielle stammered.

"Ghost, spirit, call it whatever you like. It took me a while, but I finally got you to see me." Xavier's face was smug with satisfaction.

"I don't understand any of this. You're dead. You're not supposed to be here. You're not real."

"I guess that depends on your definition of real. Just put down the lamp. We can talk."

Danielle hesitantly lowered the lamp onto the dresser. Her hands trembled.

"I've had years to think about this and I'm still not sure what's happened. All I know is that I hung around for three days until someone found my body, and I just never left. Just imagine how I've felt, stuck in this house for the last three years. Although the past year has been quite interesting." Xavier grinned. "I've had lots of time to study you. I know all about what you like."

Her face reddened again as she considered all the things he might have observed. Anger replaced her fear. She stepped forward with her hand raised, intending to smack him square across his face. Xavier grabbed her arm. The touch of his skin burned like a flame. Genuine sadness filled his eyes.

"Listen, I'm sorry. I didn't have much choice. I tried to stay away from you when you first moved in, but I was alone. I watched you and I saw how sad you were. I could feel you beginning to sense me. I couldn't stay away. I wanted you to see me. I wanted you."

Xavier released her arm and backed away. Overcome with emotion, all the pain, hurt and confusion of the past few months exploded inside her. Danielle's head pounded. Her vision blurred as she struggled to keep her feet grounded and stop herself from falling off the dark precipice of insanity.

At that moment, something inside her broke. She was tired of everything happening to her. She wanted to be in control for once and make something happen. Danielle haltingly stepped closer to Xavier.

She reached her hand up to run her fingers through the waves of his hair. Xavier towered over her. Over six feet tall, she guessed. She ran her hand down the side of his neck. Her fingers spread over the tattoo of the wing down to his bare chest. Xavier's chest rose and fell with his breath, but she felt no heartbeat. She had so many questions, but now was not the time for talk.

Her hands brushed across his skin and discovered a scar underneath his right breast. Her fingers traveled down his taut abs and rested on his hips. She saw the bulge of his penis pressed against his jeans and ran her hands over it. She heard his sharp intake of breath.

She unbuttoned his jeans, then unzipped them. As she pulled them to the floor, she went down with them and knelt in front of him. Her hands caressed his muscular legs, his penis pulsing and erect before her.

She felt powerful and reckless. Xavier's hands ruffled her hair. She held his penis in one hand and grasped it at the base. She stroked him teasingly with her fingers all the way to the tip and around his head.

Danielle leaned forward. Her tongue licked the length of him. She sucked the head into her mouth and flicked at the tip with her tongue. When she brought him in deeper, a moan escaped from his lips. His legs and ass tensed. As she fondled his balls, she pulled him farther and farther in.

Her clitoris tingled and wetness spread between her legs at the realization of him naked and in her control. She released him from her mouth and he sank to his knees before her.

"Danielle," he murmured. She stood up and undressed. His eyes devoured every inch of her. The electricity of desire radiated between them. Danielle knelt beside him on the carpet and pushed his chest back until he lay before her.

She straddled him and lowered herself onto his penis. He gazed up at her breasts and her erect nipples. His hand reached up to engulf her breast. He pinched one of her nipples between his thumb and finger. It sent a jolt through her body that made her grip around his penis tighten.

He trailed his fingers down her chest and belly and pressed his thumb against her clitoris. As she rose and fell against him, his hips lifted to meet her. The friction of his thumb against her clitoris was excruciatingly sweet.

She leaned back and opened herself to the ecstasy. Xavier's body became rigid as he came inside her and throbbed in his release. She shuddered with a powerful orgasm.

Danielle collapsed against him and Xavier's strong arms enclosed her. They lay together on the floor until Danielle rolled onto her back. Xavier curled on his side to face her and tangled his fingers in her hair so their connection would not be broken.

Danielle laughed quietly.

"Well, that was not quite the reaction I hoped for." Xavier raised his eyebrows.

"It's just that this is crazy. I'm crazy. What am I doing? I'm married and you're a ghost. I'm certifiably nuts."

Danielle replayed Matt's last message in her head and didn't know how much longer she would be married.

"Well, he's not here. I am. You can see me, touch me. I'm real, Danielle."

For the next few hours, Danielle and Xavier sat on the floor while she peppered him with questions. Could he leave the house, did he eat, did he sleep?

Xavier wanted to know when she began to feel his presence.

She was surprised at how comfortable she felt; how readily and unquestionably she accepted a ghost. Her mind wandered back to Nancy and the tarot reading. Was this what she meant when she said Danielle should trust what she saw? After a while, Danielle's stomach growled.

"I know you don't need to eat, but I'm famished."

"I'm hungry too, but my appetite is definitely not for food," Xavier said with his sly smile.

Danielle rolled her eyes and picked up her clothes on the way down to the kitchen. Xavier pulled on his jeans and followed her. He hopped up onto the counter where he watched her intently as she made herself a sandwich.

Her eyes strayed to the scar on his chest and the wing tattoo on his neck.

"So why a wing?" she asked between bites.

He raised his muscled arm to his neck. "A reminder to dream, rise above limitations, I was eighteen when I got it done."

"And the scar?"

The small red circle ringed with gray stood out on his skin. Xavier's eyes grew darker. An intense anger crossed his face as his fingers rose to the scar.

"The gunshot that killed me."

"Do you know who did it? Why?"

"It's complicated. Let's not talk about that now. There's something I need to tell you."

"Sounds serious."

"It's about your daughter."

Danielle's face went white. Her body immediately tensed.

"My daughter? What do you mean?"

Xavier gazed at Danielle with tenderness and sprang off the counter to stand in front of her. "I saw her when she died. I saw her soul leaving. She was beautiful, Danielle, just like you."

Danielle's body went limp as tears rolled down her cheeks.

"She's safe. You don't need to be sad. She knows how much you love her. I'm here. I understand." Xavier soothed her with his low voice. He cupped her face gently in his hands and kissed her tears away. Although it was crazy, Danielle felt that he knew what she had been going through. No one had understood her emotions in that way for a long time.

Matt always distanced himself from her sadness, as if it was a disease that he might catch. He did not want to be drawn into the memories. Xavier embraced her sorrow, and as he did, a weight lifted. Her grief seemed to dissolve when he accepted her completely.

Xavier gathered Danielle into his arms and effortlessly carried her up the stairs to the bedroom. He laid her gently on the bed and kissed her forehead, cheeks, and lips. His fingertips grazed her arms as he pulled her shirt over her head. He slowly removed her shorts, while his lips blazed a path down her belly and her legs.

He gazed at her intently as he stood at the foot of the bed. She drowned in the deep, black pools of his eyes. "You are mine. I won't let anything hurt you again."

He climbed between her legs and pushed them farther apart with his knees. He bent over to kiss the top of her head. As he entered her with one thrust, Danielle gasped. He filled every inch of her.

He then pulled out and Danielle squirmed beneath him with longing. He probed at the entrance to her vagina with the tip of his penis and swayed it slowly back and forth. She longed to wrap her arms across his back and pull him closer and deeper inside her.

Xavier pinned her arms to the bed with his hands so she could not move. She raised her hips and tried to get closer, but he continued to tease her with his slow pulses. She turned her head and closed her eyes as her body throbbed and ached.

"Open your eyes. Look at me. Tell me what you want."

Danielle opened her eyes and stared up at him. "I want you. Please, I need you inside me."

His eyes locked with hers as he drove his cock into her, hard, and made her gasp. He continued to thrust into her. His eyes never left her.

"Harder," she pleaded.

She moaned as she arched up toward him. He thrust deeper and deeper until she came with powerful shudders. He slowed and the pressure inside her built again as he rocked against her body. His breath came more quickly as he drove into her. They cried out with pleasure as they both came at the same time.

He lay on top of her and released her arms, which lay limp and helpless along with the rest of her exhausted body. He rolled on his side. "It's been a long day. Sleep, I'll be here when you wake up."

"Promise?"

"I'll always be here for you, always."

Danielle closed her eyes and drifted. In the back of her mind, she wondered what she would see when she woke up, but right now, fatigue won.

Xavier sat on the bed next to her, entranced by the steady rise and fall of her breasts. While she slept, the cell phone on her nightstand buzzed. Xavier picked it up and read a text from Matt.

I'm such an ass. I should never have left without talking to you. I'll make it up to you on Friday when I get home. Text me. I love you.

With eyes as cold as ice, Xavier deleted the message. He placed the phone back on the nightstand and traced his fingers down Danielle's thighs.

"I need you, Danielle. Nothing's going to come between us, nothing."

CHAPTER 6

At 11:30 a.m. the next day, Danielle finally woke up. She scanned the room and saw that she was alone. The past few days had sped by in a whirlwind. She didn't have a handle on what was real and what was not. She was in a perpetual state of imbalance. But today, she realized her grief had finally lifted. She had seen everything through the fog of loss, but now everything was clear. And she had clearly gotten herself into quite a situation. She was having an affair with a ghost.

She loved her husband, but he wasn't here and she didn't know if and when he was coming back. She didn't quite know yet what she felt for Xavier — love, lust? Was it possible to love two people at the same time? But she did know that Xavier had given her the support and understanding that Matt had been unable or unwilling to give.

She threw a sundress over her head and went to look for Xavier. Before she walked downstairs, she crossed the hallway to the baby's room. When she entered, she felt at peace. Xavier's words to her last night and his acknowledgement of her feelings had finally brought her the closure that she had longed for. She was still sad, but knew in her heart that her daughter was safe. Danielle grabbed the garbage bags from the room and kept the door open as she left.

At the bottom of the stairs, Danielle stopped. Xavier had opened the back door and stood in the doorframe with his arms braced against the wood, his body tensed and coiled like a spring about to propel forward. The muscles in his forearms rippled. Danielle's eyes traveled across his back and admired the wide muscles that tapered to his slim waist.

As Danielle watched, he dropped to one knee and pounded his fists against the doorframe. He bent his head into his hands and cursed under his breath. She waited uncomfortably as she intruded on this private moment. Despite the intimacy of the past days, he was practically a stranger. As if sensing her presence, Xavier stood and turned.

Danielle walked toward him and deposited the bags by the back door. She saw resignation and sadness on his face.

"Hey," said Danielle with the awkwardness of the morning after a one-night stand. She wanted to reach out and touch him, but held back.

Xavier stepped closer to her, placed his hand under her chin, and tilted her head up to him. He leaned down and kissed her gently. His other hand wrapped around her back and pulled her tightly against him. As his kiss intensified, Danielle melted against his chest. He took her hand and led her over to the couch.

"We need to talk. I need your help." The intensity returned to his eyes.

"My help? I don't know what I can do to help you, but sure." She wondered what he could be asking her to do.

"I've kept trying, but it's no use. I can't leave this house. It's like I'm bound here."

Danielle's heart fell just a little. Her gaze dropped down to her lap. She didn't want him to see that she might actually care if he left. The idea upset her more than she liked to admit.

"I didn't realize you wanted to leave." She tried to sound nonchalant.

Xavier held her hands. "There's someone I need to see. That's what I need you to help me with."

Danielle pictured some sophisticated, New York model that Xavier couldn't bear to be without, even in death. Her mind worked overtime. Was that all this was? Xavier just sweetening her up so she would be willing to do anything for him? She felt stupid for letting it bother her so much.

Danielle pulled her hands from his, and placed them under her legs. She looked up at him and swallowed her pride.

"I need to see my brother. I need you to make something up to get him over here. I have to try to talk to him."

"Your brother?" Relief flooded her chest.

"He's my younger brother. I've always taken care of him and tried to look out for him." Xavier ran his hand through his hair and shook his head. "He's had a hard time. I was trying to help him, but now I've left him alone. I need him to know that it wasn't his fault. I need to make sure he's going to be okay."

"His fault? Do you mean the shooting?"

Xavier nodded. "Caleb had gotten mixed up in drugs. He owed this guy a lot of money. I told him I'd pay it off if he agreed to go to rehab. Caleb was supposed to come over to get the money. His dealer showed up instead. When I refused to give him the money and wanted to know where Caleb was, he pulled out a gun, shot me, and took the money. It all happened so quickly. I collapsed on the floor and the next thing I knew I was staring at my body wondering what the hell was going on. I need to see my brother and try to talk to him."

"Oh my God. Of course I'll do it. I'm so sorry." Danielle suddenly remembered the fact that she was talking to a ghost. "But will he be able to see you?"

"I don't know, but I need to try. I need you to call him. Tell him you found some of my things and that you want to give them to him. He'll want the money he can get selling the photographs. Ask him to come over to the house."

"I'll do it right now. What's his number?"

"Wait, not yet." Xavier's eyes became desperate and wild. "I don't want anything to change between us. I think that's the reason that I'm here, for us to be together somehow. I know you, Danielle. I know you down to your core. We're connected. I know it's complicated, but we're meant to be together."

"I don't know what you want me to say. I'm just really confused right now."

"I know how you feel about me. I can see it in your eyes and the way you look at me. I can feel it in your body."

"I haven't had time to think. There's Matt. Besides, it's not like you have unlimited options at the moment. And there's that other minor wrinkle of the fact that you're a ghost, which probably makes me certifiably insane."

Xavier reached up and put a finger to her lips. "I am your destiny. You can't deny it. Let me show you."

He pulled Danielle onto his lap. Her legs straddled him. His hands gripped her hips tightly as he pulled her closer. Warmth radiated between her legs. His hands slid under her dress and rose up her thighs. Xavier's mouth turned up in a wry smile when he realized the only thing underneath her dress was her bare skin.

He drew her forward. When their lips met, the electricity crackled between them. His kisses grew more insistent and his tongue found hers. She draped her arms around his neck. He moved one hand around her waist, then held her securely as he stood. Danielle wrapped her legs around him.

He carried her to the dining room and brought her to the table. He pulled her legs from around his back and lifted her dress over her hips. He unzipped his jeans, let them fall to the floor, and then put his hand against her chest.

"I feel your heart beating. It's beating for me. Look at me and tell me you want me to go. Tell me you don't want me." Xavier leaned close to her mouth.

Without waiting for an answer, he grabbed her legs and looped them across his broad shoulders. He kneeled and bent his head toward her crotch and murmured against her skin.

"We belong together. I'll never leave you. I know you want me."

She couldn't even comprehend his words. His breath and his lips on her skin distracted her from all logic. Her body contracted until she was on the brink of an orgasm.

Xavier rose and lowered her legs from his shoulders. His hand slipped between her legs. One finger glided into her and pulled out as she pressed against him. He brought his finger to his mouth, deliberately licking it. Then he pressed his lips against hers in an ardent kiss.

"Tell me to stop, and I will. What do you want?"

She couldn't think or speak. How could she with his hard, naked body in front of her? His eyes saw through all of her indecision to her core. She leaned back on the table and searched for an answer in his face.

"Do you want me to go?"

She silently shook her head. Xavier placed his hands on her hips as she wound her legs around him.

"You're never going to want anyone else." He entered her.

Danielle inhaled as he filled her. Her back arched and her hands gripped the sides of the table. As he thrust inside her, his eyes never left her face. He quickened his pace and pulled her hips toward him with one hand. He placed his other hand on her stomach.

He drove into her harder and harder until she spilled over the edge and came in waves against him as he emptied himself into her. He lifted her up until she faced him; their bodies entwined. Their skin shimmered with sweat. As she kissed his shoulder, she tasted the salt of his skin. At this moment, Xavier was right; she couldn't imagine wanting anyone else but him.

CHAPTER 7

After untangling her body from his, Danielle went to get her phone.

When Xavier was with her, everything seemed clear, but away from him, she doubted herself and guilt crept in like a shadow. Did she still have a life with Matt? Was she willing to give up her life for a ghost? Nothing made sense. She wished she could talk to Karen about this, but would she listen? Would she actually believe her?

She would help Xavier with his brother. Then maybe she needed to go away for a few days by herself, without Xavier or Matt, and think about what to do. She checked her phone and still half expected to see a message from Matt. It made it easier to rationalize her infidelity when there was still no word from him.

She came downstairs. Thankfully, Xavier had put his pants back on. He was enough of a distraction half-dressed. She studied the curves of his chest and the trail of dark hair that continued below the waistband of his jeans, then licked her lips and imagined her tongue following that path.

"Danielle, you okay? See something you like?" Xavier laughed.

"What? Sorry. Just thinking about what I'm going to say to Caleb. I got my phone. Give me Caleb's number and let's do this." Danielle dialed the number that Xavier gave her. Grateful that Caleb didn't answer, she left a message. "This is Danielle Williams. We bought your brother's old house and I got your number from the real estate agent. We found some of your brother's photographs when we were cleaning up the attic and wanted to give them to you. We'd love it if you could stop by tonight and pick them up. Just come over, or you can call me at this number. Thanks."

The rest of the afternoon, they wandered aimlessly around the house and waited for a return phone call. Xavier was lost in his thoughts of his brother. Danielle contemplated the state of her marriage. She also worried about what would happen if this didn't work, and Caleb was not able to see Xavier. They both became restless as they waited for the phone to ring. The sunset saturated the sky with a deep red as time dragged slowly by.

Driven crazy by the endless wait, Danielle went up to the attic and retrieved her sketchbook and pencils.

"Since we're just waiting around, I'm going to draw you. So go sit down over there against the wall."

"I like it when you order me around. Should I get undressed?"

"Just sit down and stop talking, so I can get your face right." Danielle sat down in front of him and opened her sketchbook to a blank page. She observed the lines and angles, the light and shadow of his face. She started with the black pools of his eyes that always pulled her in.

"You're very sexy when you're concentrating like that."

"Just please be quiet. I'm trying to work here."

When she finished, she ripped the page from the sketchbook and handed it to Xavier. Inside his dark pupils, she had added the reflection of her own green eyes.

"It's beautiful. Thank you. I love it."

Danielle opened the door to the porch and let in the cool air. She stepped outside. Stars shone in the cloudless sky. She sat in the doorway and drew her knees to her chest. Xavier came and sat behind her. She rested her head against his shoulder.

As she leaned against him, his strength supported her. They didn't talk, but a peacefulness settled between them. She placed her hands on the floor, and he reached his hands behind to intertwine his fingers with hers.

When she closed her eyes, she felt a palpable energy flow between them. Deep in her heart, she knew that they lingered in the eye of a storm. Only a slight shift would cause them to career out of control.

"Do you think he'll just show up?" Danielle asked.

Xavier just shrugged. "I don't know. Anything's possible, I guess."

They both jumped when the telephone rang. Danielle stumbled up and ran to answer it before it went to voice mail.

"Hello?"

"Hey, I'm glad you picked up," said Karen. "Matt called me. He's all in a panic because you never answered his text. He's on his way back from Las Vegas. He'll probably be there tonight."

"What? Tonight? What are you talking about? I didn't get a text." Danielle's heart began to race, and she had troubling catching her breath.

"Yeah, he went on and on about how sorry he was. What's up with you? I thought you'd be happy to hear he was coming home. What, you got your lover over there or something?" Karen joked.

"Listen, I've got to go." Danielle hung up on Karen. She scrolled through her phone to find Matt's text.

"Was that Caleb?" Xavier walked toward her.

"No, it was Karen. Apparently Matt is on his way back. Tonight. I don't what happened. I didn't get his text."

"Yeah, about that." Xavier looked at her sheepishly. "I kind of deleted it from your phone."

"You what?" Danielle shouted. She took a deep breath. "You're monitoring my phone? What gives you the right? Now what are we going to do? What am I going to do? Your brother's on his way here. Matt's on his way here. I'm not ready for this. I'm fucked."

"I was just trying to protect you. You finally seemed happy here with me. I thought you needed some time to explore your options. I didn't know he was coming back. You knew this would happen eventually. You knew you would have to make a choice."

"But not tonight. Tonight! In a matter of hours. I can't do this."

The doorbell rang.

"Shit!" Danielle exclaimed.

"Just relax. I'll stay out of your way, but I'll be here. I'll always be here for you."

As she walked to the door, beads of sweat trickled down her forehead and she felt light-headed. Then she began to think logically. Matt would not ring the doorbell in his own house. She peered through the peephole and sighed in relief.

"Come over here. I think it's your brother."

Xavier looked through the peephole. "That's him."

As Danielle opened the door, Xavier retreated to the living room. Caleb was shorter than Xavier and more slightly built. He appeared to be in his early twenties. His dark hair was wavy like Xavier's, but cut short. He wore a polo shirt and khakis, definitely more preppy than Xavier. He had the same dark eyes as Xavier, but his were bloodshot and glassy.

"You must be Caleb."

"Yeah, I'm Caleb." He looked around nervously.

"Come on in. Let's go in the living room."

"Thanks." Caleb followed her into the house.

As they entered the living room, Xavier stood in the corner. The pain of seeing his brother turned his face into a morbid mask.

Caleb sat on the couch and scanned the room. He licked his lips and rubbed his nose repeatedly. One knee twitched up and down. Danielle sat across from him. Her anxiety increased with each second that passed.

"So you said you had some things that belonged to my brother. Where are they?"

"Okay, listen, Caleb. This is kind of difficult to explain, so I'm just going to come right out with it. Your brother's here, He wants to talk to you." Danielle watched as the expression on Caleb's face turned frantic and he stood up.

"What the fuck are you talking about? Is this some kind of joke?" Caleb shouted.

"Just calm down. Xavier, please come over here," Danielle implored.

"Who are you talking to? Is this some kind of setup? I knew I shouldn't have come here," yelled Caleb. His face reddened as he glared at Danielle.

Xavier stood in front of Caleb, but Caleb looked deliriously past him and reached around to his back.

"Caleb, Caleb it's me. You've got to see me," Xavier pleaded as he grabbed Caleb's shoulders. Caleb walked straight through him and left Xavier standing defeated. His head hung down.

"Try again. Caleb, he's right behind you," said Danielle.

Caleb whirled around and faced Danielle again. His body shook and his wild eyes darted around the room.

"Who the fuck are you talking to? Who put you up to this?"

"No one, really. Please calm down. Xavier, a little help here?" Danielle turned toward Xavier, who stood across the room, stunned.

"He doesn't see me," Xavier whispered with resignation.

"I don't know what kind of game you're playing here. My brother is dead!" Caleb pulled a pistol from the back of his pants. "Now give me his stuff and I'll get out of here."

Fuck, thought Danielle as she put her hands up in front of her. "Okay, okay, just give me a minute." She looked helplessly at Xavier, who had stepped over to Caleb's side. He placed his arm on Caleb's shoulder, but he drifted through Caleb's flesh and blood like a shadow. Danielle realized there would be nothing that Xavier could do to stop his brother or protect her.

"Be careful, Danielle. He's obviously high. Just tell him you're going to go to get my things. Try to get to the front door and run."

"I'm going to go get your brother's things." Danielle backed away from Caleb. At that moment, she heard the sound of a car pull in the driveway. *Matt*, thought Danielle. Relief and terror struck her at the same time.

"Who the fuck is that?" Caleb pointed the gun at Danielle.

"It's my husband. Just put the gun down. You can leave. We'll just forget all about this."

"No, no way. You're up to something. Did Vigo set this up? Is this about the money?"

Matt opened the door and walked into the foyer. "Hey, Danielle, whose car is that—" Matt stopped mid-sentence as he entered the living room. "What the hell?"

"Just back up, or I swear to God I'll shoot both of you." Caleb's hand shook as he swung the gun back and forth from Danielle to Matt. Beads of sweat dripped down his forehead.

Danielle looked at Matt with desperation in her eyes. Xavier stood helplessly. Every muscle in his body tensed.

Matt stepped closer to Danielle. "Just let her leave, and we'll figure this out. What do you want? Money? Whatever you want you can have."

"No way, you'll call the police," said Caleb.

"He's desperate, Danielle. I can see it. You need to run toward Matt, toward the door," Xavier pleaded. She stumbled as Xavier pushed her toward Matt.

"Oh my God, are you crazy?" Danielle forgot that no one else could hear Xavier.

"Who are you calling crazy?" Caleb strode toward Danielle with the gun.

Matt suddenly rushed forward, in front of Danielle. She heard the crack of the gun and Matt crumpled to the floor in front of her. The next few seconds unfolded frame by frame. Each horror stretched out endlessly.

Caleb stared at his hands as if they were not connected to his body. Terror distorted his face as he ran from the house.

Danielle kneeled next to Matt. The blood pooled around him and gushed from the wide gash in his neck.

"No, Matt, no!" Danielle screamed. She grabbed her phone and dialed 911 as she hurried back to his side.

Danielle flinched at the sound of another gunshot. *Caleb*, she thought, as her chest heaved. Turning her head, she looked at Xavier. The torment on his face echoed her own.

"I'm so sorry. I should never have left." Matt's strength diminished with each labored breath.

"No, shh…it's okay. The ambulance will be here soon. Just hang on."

"I love you. Never doubt that I loved you."

"I love you too, just stay with me, stay with me." Danielle sobbed as she pressed her hands against his neck and tried to stop the bleeding.

Matt suddenly gazed over Danielle's shoulder. A question formed in his eyes.

"Who is that?" he murmured in a barely audible voice.

Danielle turned and saw Xavier standing behind her. He shook his head.

"No, no. Stay here with me. Please don't go." Matt's body went limp in her arms and his eyes froze. Danielle collapsed over Matt's lifeless body as Xavier walked away.

CHAPTER 8

D anielle sat in her car outside the house and gathered the courage to go inside. She had not been back to the house since the night when Matt and Caleb died. The past few weeks had been numbing. Flashes of memory sparked in her mind—the blaring lights of the ambulance, the police, blood on her hands, Caleb's body on the front lawn, and Matt's lifeless eyes.

She had been staying with Karen and Brian for over a month. Karen, with her usual single-mindedness, had taken over and led Danielle through the interviews with the police, the funeral arrangements, and ultimately the funeral.

But Danielle knew it was time to go. She woke up screaming nearly every night, except when she dreamed of Xavier. His dark eyes calmed her and kept the nightmares at bay.

Danielle had finally gotten in touch with her mother a week ago. She was off on her latest crusade saving whales in Iceland. She had responded with her usual lack of maternal instinct saying she was so sorry, but that she really couldn't make it back to Fairview to see her right now. Wasn't it good that Danielle had such wonderful friends to take care of her? She would be okay, right? *Right*, thought Danielle.

She had also resigned from her teaching job. She couldn't bear the reminders that slammed her in the face everywhere she went in this town. She felt poisonous to everything and everyone.

After she packed up a few of her things at the house, she was going to drive directly to the airport. She didn't know how long she would be gone, or if she would ever come back. Karen had tried to convince her not to go, but Danielle knew that she had no choice.

Danielle placed her key in the lock and pushed the door open. The silent memories of the house overwhelmed her. She avoided the living room and went straight up to the bedroom to pack her clothes. She hoped she could get in and out quickly and avoid Xavier.

Danielle placed her suitcase on top of the bed. She pulled clothes from the closet and threw them inside. When she had just about everything packed, she glanced at her nightstand. The envelope she had found in the attic with Xavier's picture was still there. She stuffed it at the bottom of the suitcase underneath her clothes.

She then grabbed the pack of tarot cards from her nightstand and picked up the last card she had pulled from the deck, the Lovers. She shuffled the deck and pulled out another card, the Eight of Cups. The figure had his back turned and walked away across the water alone. That was just what she needed to do, she thought as she jammed the card in the pocket of her jeans. She needed to turn her back and walk away from all this heartache. She put the rest of the deck in her suitcase. Her back to the door, she sensed Xavier even before she turned around.

"Xavier," Danielle whispered. She had to stop herself from running into his arms and allowing him to comfort her. When she looked into his eyes, her body trembled. She would never forget his eyes. Both of their faces now reflected the darkness of the same tragic mirror.

"I've been waiting for you," said Xavier. His voice broke with pain.

"I'm just here to pick up some of my things, then I'm leaving." Danielle could not face him when she spoke.

Xavier walked toward her.

"You can't pretend that I'm a stranger. You can't pretend that none of this happened."

"You know I can't stay here. I need some time away from everyone. I'm so sorry about your brother."

Xavier strode toward her and cradled her face in his hands. "None of this is your fault. I want you to remember that."

"Of course it's my fault. If it wasn't for me, Matt and your brother would still be alive."

"You can't think that way. Sometimes things happen that are out of our control. I'm the one who started this whole mess, but finding you was worth it. There has to be a reason that I met you. I won't let you go. We will be together. I'll find a way. Wherever you are, I will find you." Xavier spoke with unwavering conviction.

He kissed her fiercely. Danielle longed to lose herself in his burning embrace. It would be so easy to drift into his world of shadows and dreams with one foot in death and one in life.

She pulled away and lowered his hands from her face. "I can't stay." Danielle zipped up her suitcase. She knew the only way to leave would be to go now and not turn back. She could not look up at him again. She didn't have the strength.

Danielle lifted her suitcase from the bed and lugged it down the stairs. When she got into her car and closed the door behind her, she allowed herself one last glance up at the bedroom. Xavier stood at the window. His eyes locked with hers. She felt their familiar pull and the desire to abandon everything and sink into his arms.

Danielle swallowed hard. Her heart shattered in more ways than she thought possible. She backed the car down the driveway. Eyes still up at the window, she watched as Xavier turned away.

Danielle knew she would always be bound to Xavier, but her ties to him were laced with blood and death: her daughter, Matt, Caleb. As she drove away, the memories tried to draw her back toward the house, back to Xavier.

She needed to get far enough away that those memories would snap and break. As she continued down the road, she had no idea what the future would hold; she only hoped she could outrun her past.

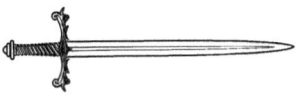

The Eight of Cups card holds disappointment and withdrawal. Will the presence of Xavier taint her new life? The Hanged Man card foretells letting go and sacrifice. Danielle must become stronger and follow her future to find…what?

Coming this fall: follow Danielle's journey in *Eight of Cups*, Book 2 and *The Hanged Man*, Book 3 in The Tarot Trilogy.

FROM THE AUTHOR

Thank you for reading *Three of Swords*! If you enjoyed it, I would be thrilled if you would consider telling a friend or leaving a review. For updates and news about upcoming books, follow me on Twitter @JDBrettonWriter, or connect with me by email at BrettonJD@gmailcom. I'd love to hear from you!

J.D. Bretton